# HOW TO GROW A DINOSAUR

For Grace, who taught me everything I know about dinosaurs,
and for Phoebe, who wanted to grow her own chickens! – C.H.

For Mum and Dad – E.E.

**SIMON AND SCHUSTER**
First published in Great Britain in 2011 by Simon and Schuster UK Ltd
1st Floor, 222 Gray's Inn Road, London WC1X 8HB
A CBS Company

Text copyright © 2011 Caryl Hart (www.carylhart.com)
Illustrations copyright © 2011 Edward Eaves

The right of Caryl Hart and Edward Eaves to be identified as the
author and illustrator of this work has been asserted by them in
accordance with the Copyright, Designs and Patents Act, 1988

A CIP catalogue record for this book is available from the
British Library upon request

PB ISBN: 978-1-84738-594-9
eBook ISBN: 978-0-85707-636-6

Printed in China
20 19 18 17 16 15 14 13 12 11

The inclusion of author or illustrator website addresses in
this book does not constitute an endorsement by or an
association with Simon and Schuster UK Ltd
of such sites or the content, products,
advertising or other materials
presented on such sites.

# HOW TO GROW A
# DINOSAUR

# CARYL HART AND ED EAVES

**SIMON AND SCHUSTER**
London   New York   Sydney

**Hooray!**
Today is a brilliant, sun-shiny day.
I can play in my paddling pool,
and ride my bike, and build a den!

I pull on my shorts and T-shirt and rush out into the garden. Then . . .

"Albie!"

It's Mum. She has a basket of tools in one hand
and some packets of seeds in the other.
I know EXACTLY what this means – **gardening!**

I HATE gardening!

But Mum says, "Come on, Albie,
let's make a vegetable patch."

All day long I weed and dig. It's SOOOO hot!
"Can't we finish now?" I groan.

"Just as soon as you've planted these," says Mum.
She hands me some seeds. "You might grow
something REALLY exciting!" she says.

I rip open the packets and fling
the seeds over the soil.

DONE!

The next morning, I open my window.
What's going on?
Outside is a JUNGLE!

This is CRAZY!

I race out into the garden and . . .

# WOOOAAAHHH!

I tumble into a hole, a very STRANGE hole.
It looks like a GIGANTIC animal's footprint.

But that's just silly –
the only creature that big would be . . .

# A dinosaur!

# AARRRGGGHH!

It's a
**HUGE**
Tyrannosaurus
Rex –
and I think it's HUNGRY!

I dive into a tangle of creepers.
The dinosaur thunders past and disappears.

That was close!
This place is scary. I want to go home –
and I'm HUNGRY too!

I spot some brightly-coloured beans dangling from a branch. They smell amazing. But can I eat them? Then I notice a seed packet on the ground . . .

JELLYBEAN TREE EDIBLE FRUIT!

FAST GROWING!

# YIPPEE!
I knew it! They're jellybeans!
## YUM!

# This is **mad!**

Jungles **don't** grow overnight!
Jellybeans **don't** grow on trees!

## Dinosaurs are EXTINCT!

I wonder . . .
I rummage in my pocket.

**TRIASSIC JUNGLE**

GROW YOUR OWN INSTANT
PREHISTORIC LANDSCAPE

**CRIKEY!** In my rush to plant those seeds, I didn't even look at the packets . . .

EASY-TO-GROW
TYRANNOSAURUS
REX

FEED WELL

DINOSAUR
MIX

SCATTER ON THE
GROUND AND
TAKE COVER!

Dinosaur **MIX!??**

That means there are **more** of them!

Suddenly, something grabs my T-shirt
and drags me up, up, up into the air.
SCREEEEECCCHHHH!
It's a giant Pterodactyl!

Heeellp!

It drops me into a nest high up in the jellybean tree. Three hungry chicks peck my feet. "Don't eat **me!**" I shout. "Eat **these!**" I throw them a handful of jellybeans.

Then . . .

GRAAAAARRRGGGHHH!

A terrifying roar fills the air.

The T-rex is right below me!
He's having a fight with a stegosaurus.

## It's a real, live dino-battle!

I lean over to get a closer look . . .

. . . but the tree starts to sway, and the T-rex looks up! He glares straight at me, sniffs the air, and licks his lips.

Uh-oh! Time to go!

I jump out of the nest but the T-rex opens his terrible jaws and . . . CHOMP! His teeth sink into the branch.

I run for my life . . .

PHEW! There's my house . . .

I dive into my room, slamming the window shut behind me. **MADE IT!**

But now Mum is calling. "Albie! Let's water your seeds!"

OH NO!
I race downstairs to stop her going out, but it's too late.

"Oh, Albie," she gasps . . .

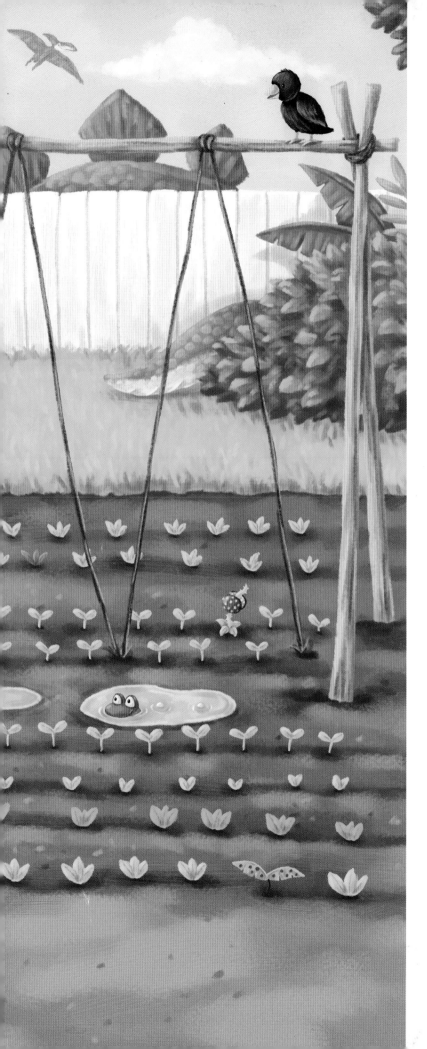

"It's beautiful!
Just scatter a few more
seeds over here and it
will be **perfect**."

Uh-oh . . .